Published by Penguin Books Australia Ltd, 1999

©Disney/Pixar

Illustrated by the storybook artists at Disney Publishing Creative Development

Mr Potato Head® is a registered trademark of Hasbro, Inc.
Used with permission ©Hasbro, Inc. All Rights Reserved.
Slinky® Dog ©James Industries.
Etch A Sketch® ©The Ohio Art Company

Printed and bound in Hong Kong

0 7214 8735 1

1 3 5 7 9 10 8 6 4 2

It was playtime in Andy's room, and the toys were cutting loose, the way they always did when there were no humans around.

Rex the dinosaur and Buzz the space ranger were playing the Buzz Lightyear video game.

'Go, Buzz!' Rex cried. 'Maybe this time we'll actually win!'

But just then the evil Emperor Zurg destroyed Buzz onscreen.

'I'll never defeat Zurg,' Buzz said with a sigh.

Meanwhile, Woody was busy getting ready to go to Cowboy Camp with Andy. Cowboy Camp was Woody's favourite annual event, and the toy cowboy was just plain excited.

Suddenly Andy burst into the room to play. The toys froze. Andy went straight to Woody and Buzz. But, just as Andy was having the two toys do their super wild-west handshake, Woody's arm ripped!

Andy wanted his mother to repair Woody's arm, but she put Woody on a high shelf instead. 'I'll fix him later,' she said as she placed Woody next to a long-lost penguin squeaky toy named Wheezy.

From his perch on the shelf, Woody sadly sat with Wheezy and watched Andy's mum drive Andy off to camp without him.

'We're all just one stitch away from a garage sale anyway,' Wheezy said with a sigh.

Sure enough, Wheezy was right. A little while later, Mrs. Davis came into Andy's room and chose Wheezy for a garage sale!

'I've got to save Wheezy!' Woody cried to the other toys. He quickly whistled for Buster, Andy's dog. Then he rode the pup down to the garage sale and grabbed onto Wheezy. 'Now take us back to Andy's room,' Woody told Buster. But, before they reached the doggie door, Woody's torn arm gave out. The cowboy tumbled to the ground.

A greedy human hand instantly reached out to grab him.

Poor Woody! He had saved Wheezy, but now he was in danger! The toys in Andy's room looked out the window and watched in horror as the man who had grabbed Woody ran to his car.

'He's stealing Woody!' Buzz yelled. Buzz jumped from the window, slid down the drain pipe, and raced toward the car. But he was too late. The car sped away, with Woody inside. All Buzz could see was the car's licence plate — LZTYBRN — and a single chicken feather floating in the air.

A little while later, Al McWhiggin reached his apartment across the street from Al's Toy Barn. Al was the man who had stolen Woody. He was the owner of Al's Toy Barn, and he hoped to sell Woody for lots of money. He hastily locked Woody in a special display case and made a quick telephone call.

Then, dressed in the Al's Toy Barn chicken suit, he headed across the street to film another TV commercial for his store.

As soon as Al left the room, Woody ran to look for a way to escape. Suddenly a happy-go-lucky toy horse popped from a box and happily licked Woody on the check. Seconds later, Jessie, a cowgirl doll, crawled from her box.

'Howdy!' she said to Woody. Then she turned to Bullseye. 'Be a good horse, and help Prospector greet our new friend.'

Bullseye quickly pushed a sealed toy box toward Woody. A wise-looking old Prospector doll waved and smiled out at Woody.

All three toys seemed so delighted to see Woody that he felt a little guilty when he told them he just wanted to go home to Andy.

'You can't go!' Jessie exclaimed. 'You're our leader, Woody.'

'How do you know my name?' Woody gasped. As he backed away, he saw a stack of comic books. All the covers had pictures of his face! 'That's me!' he exclaimed.

'You don't know who you are, do you?' the Prospector said. Quickly he nodded to Jessie, and she turned on a television.

'It's Woody's Roundup!' a cheery voice on the TV announced.
'Starring Jessic, the yodelling cowgirl...Stinky Pete the
Prospector...Bullseye the horse...and Sher-r-r-riff Woody!'

Woody couldn't believe it! He had been a television star!

'Now, you're part of a very collectible set — us!' the
Prospector explained. 'Al is selling us to a museum in Japan.'

Meanwhile, back in Andy's room, Buzz was leading the other toys in an effort to figure out who had taken Woody.

'LZTYBRN,' Buzz announced. 'That licence plate is our key to finding Woody.' Suddenly Buzz put the letters together. 'Al's Toy Barn! The man who took Woody was Al from Al's Toy Barn!'

Buzz turned to Etch and had him make a map. Then Buzz revealed his plan. 'I'm going to Al's Toy Barn to rescue Woody.'

Buzz was determined to save his cowboy pal. 'Woody once risked his life to save me. I can't call myself his friend if I'm not willing to do the same.'

'I'm coming with you,' Slinky announced. Rex, Hamm and Mr. Potato Head quickly followed the lead.

In the quiet of the night, Buzz and his friends climbed out the bedroom window and crept across the rooftop. Their rescue mission had begun.

At the edge of the rooftop, Slinky held on with his paws as one by one, the toys used his coils to bungee jump to the ground. When everyone was safely down, Buzz looked back up at the toys waiting and watching in the window above.

'To Al's Toy Barn — and Beyond!' he shouted bravely.

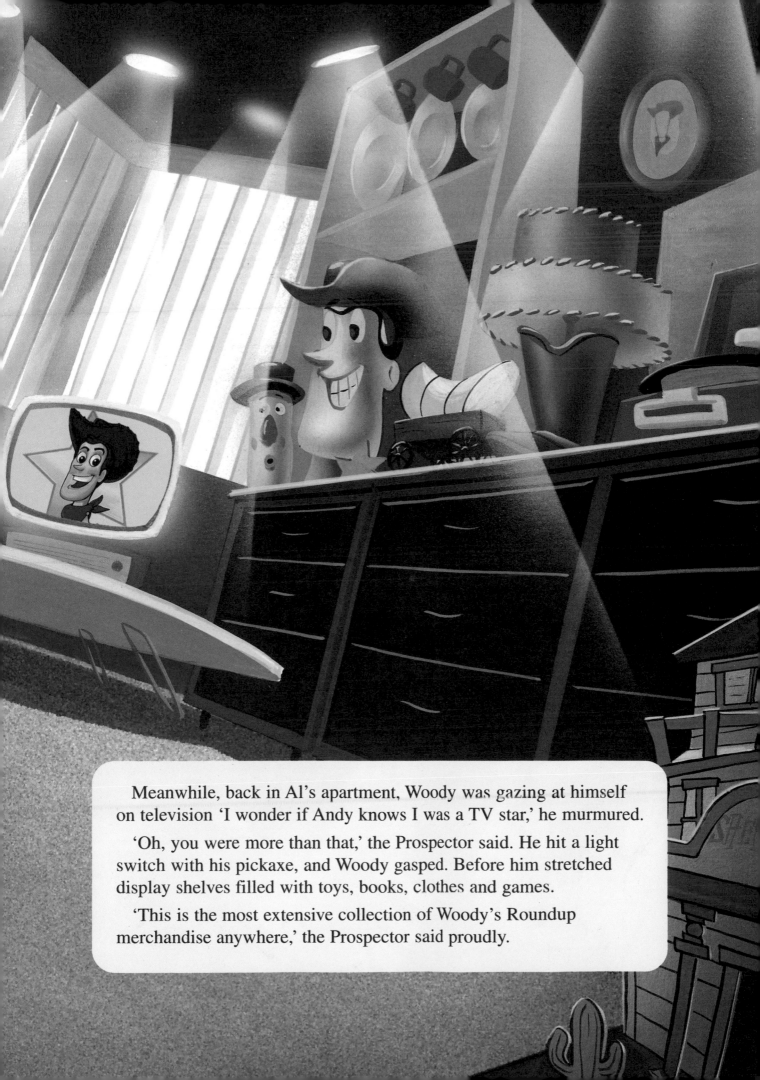

Meanwhile, back in Al's apartment, Woody was gazing at himself on television 'I wonder if Andy knows I was a TV star,' he murmured.

'Oh, you were more than that,' the Prospector said. He hit a light switch with his pickaxe, and Woody gasped. Before him stretched display shelves filled with toys, books, clothes and games.

'This is the most extensive collection of Woody's Roundup merchandise anywhere,' the Prospector said proudly.

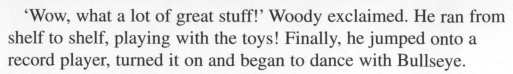

'Wow, what a lot of great stuff!' Woody exclaimed. He ran from shelf to shelf, playing with the toys! Finally, he jumped onto a record player, turned it on and began to dance with Bullseye.

'We're not supposed to play!' Jessie shouted. But after a while, even Jessie couldn't resist. She leaped onto the record player and began dancing with Woody and Bullseye as they spun around.

When Al came home, he picked up Woody to put him on a display stand, but Woody's arm caught on the stand and tore off! 'Oh no!' Al gasped. He put the torn arm in his pocket and quickly went to his telephone. He called the Cleaner to come and fix Woody first thing the next morning.

Woody couldn't leave without his arm, so he waited until Al fell asleep on the couch and went to get his arm from Al's pocket. Suddenly, Woody looked down and saw Bullseye licking Al's fingers! 'Cut that out!' he hissed. 'You'll wake him up!'

But Al woke up anyway and put Woody back in his display case.

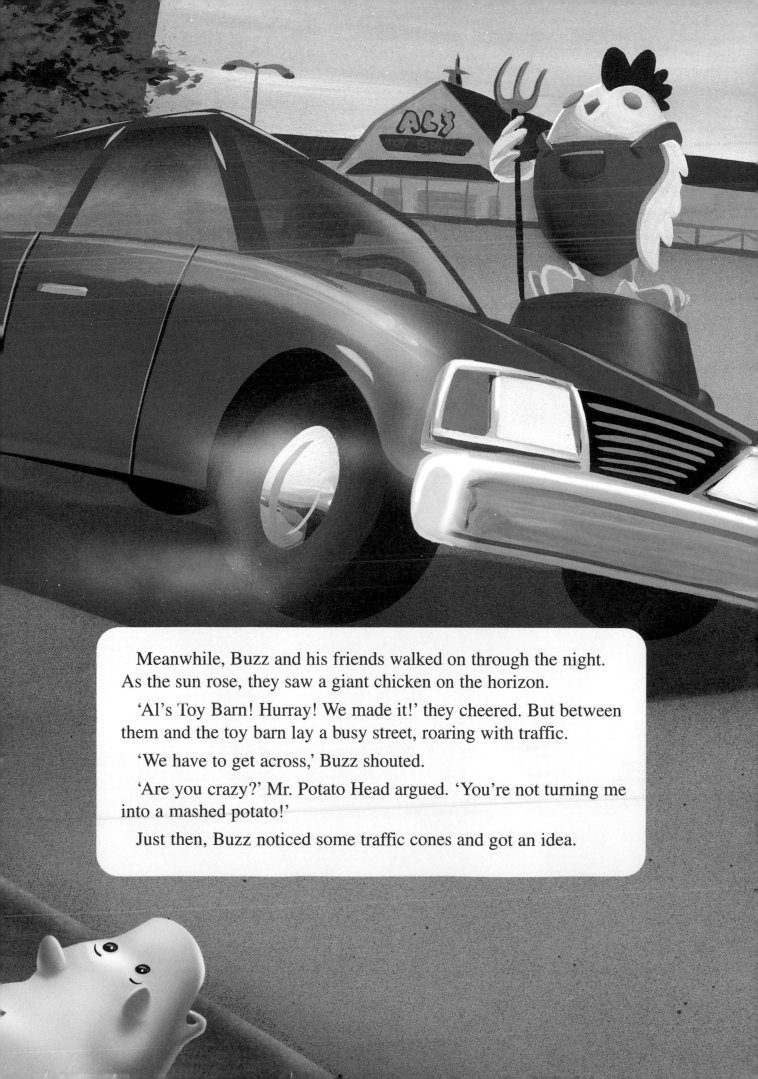

Meanwhile, Buzz and his friends walked on through the night. As the sun rose, they saw a giant chicken on the horizon.

'Al's Toy Barn! Hurray! We made it!' they cheered. But between them and the toy barn lay a busy street, roaring with traffic.

'We have to get across,' Buzz shouted.

'Are you crazy?' Mr. Potato Head argued. 'You're not turning me into a mashed potato!'

Just then, Buzz noticed some traffic cones and got an idea.

The toys pulled the traffic cones over their heads and dashed into the street.

SCREEEECH! Cars swerved around the cones.

'Go!' Buzz yelled. Just then, Mr. Potato Head's shoe got stuck in a wad of chewing gum. As he struggled to pull free, a truck thundered past, spilling a load of concrete pipes. The pipes rolled directly toward Mr. Potato Head. At the last second, he yanked his shoe loose and ran.

At last, the toys made it across the road. 'Good job, troops!'
Buzz said. 'Excellent covert manoeuvring. Let's keep moving.'

In the street, cars and trucks smashed into each other, bounced
off traffic barriers, and knocked down street lights. But the toys
hurried across the parking lot toward Al's Toy Barn, ignoring the
honking horns and screeching brakes behind them.

At the same time, the Cleaner arrived at Al's apartment. 'Oh my!' he muttered when he saw Woody. 'What a classic!' Eagerly, the Cleaner opened his amazing portable toy repair kit and set to work.

Before long, Woody looked brand-new.

'You're top-notch collectible quality now,' the Prospector said after Al and the Cleaner left.

'Yep!' Woody answered. 'And I'm all ready to go home!'

Bullseye and Jessie watched sadly as Woody prepared to leave. 'You don't understand about Andy,' Woody tried to explain.

'Yes, I do,' Jessie replied sulkily. 'I belonged to a little girl once. She played with me every day — until she grew up. Then I ended up in a donations box. Even the greatest kids outgrow their toys.'

Woody couldn't believe what he was hearing. Could Andy actually outgrow Woody and give him away? Woody started believing he might really be better off in a museum, after all.

Meanwhile, Woody's pals were looking up at the hundreds of toy shelves that towered in front of them inside Al's Toy Barn.

'How will we ever find Woody in here?' Rex whined.

'We'll split up and meet in the back,' Buzz commanded.

As his friends scattered, Buzz looked around. A green light glowed from a nearby aisle. Cautiously, Buzz approached.

Before him stood an awesome display featuring a new Buzz Lightyear. And the new Buzz was wearing an amazing utility pack, complete with grappling hook, string, magnets and magnetic radials.

'I could use that!' thought Buzz.

WHAP! Suddenly a hand clenched Buzz's. It was New Buzz! 'Space Rangers are to remain in hyper-sleep until awakened by authoriscd personnel. You are breaking ranks, Ranger,' New Buzz shouted.

'Let me tell you a secret,' Buzz said, pulling away, 'You're not a Space Ranger. You're a toy!'

'Hiyaahh!' New Buzz yelled, tackling Buzz and throwing him to the floor. Their helmets crashed and their spaceboots thudded as the two space heroes clashed and tangled.

Finally, New Buzz overpowered Buzz. He twist-tied Andy's toy into a box and crammed it on a shelf. Buzz was trapped.

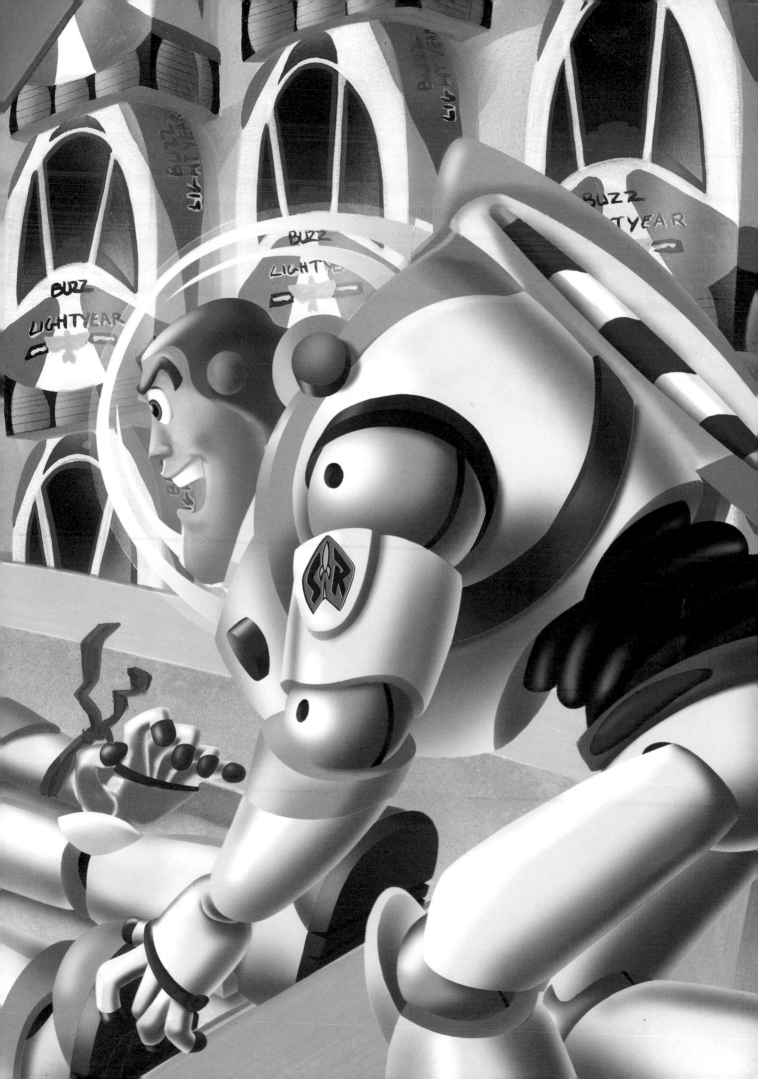

Meanwhile, in another region of Al's Toy Barn, Rex had stumbled upon a brand-new Buzz Lightyear video game manual. 'Hey, Buzz!' Rex shouted as he and the others careened up to New Buzz in a brand-new sports car. 'I found a Buzz Lightyear video strategy manual. And it reveals the secret of defeating Zurg!'

New Buzz jumped into the car. If these strange creatures knew how to defeat Zurg, New Buzz wanted to be with them.

'You've got the wrong Buzz!' shouted Andy's Buzz, but no one heard him.

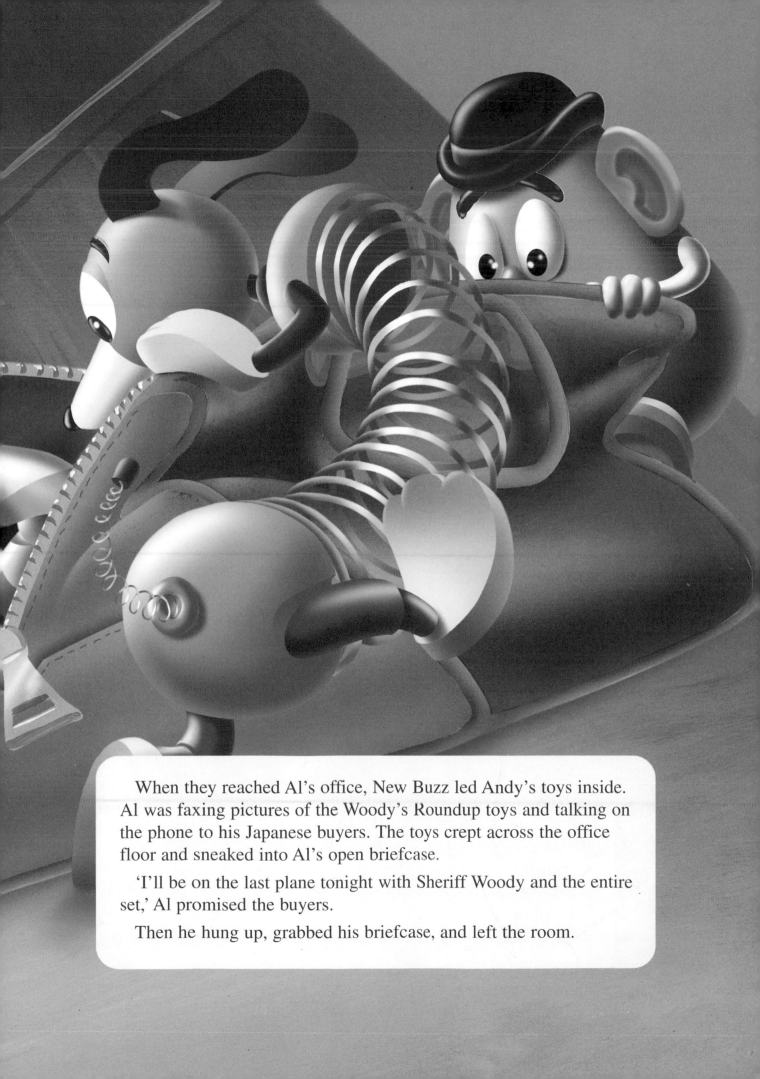

When they reached Al's office, New Buzz led Andy's toys inside. Al was faxing pictures of the Woody's Roundup toys and talking on the phone to his Japanese buyers. The toys crept across the office floor and sneaked into Al's open briefcase.

'I'll be on the last plane tonight with Sheriff Woody and the entire set,' Al promised the buyers.

Then he hung up, grabbed his briefcase, and left the room.

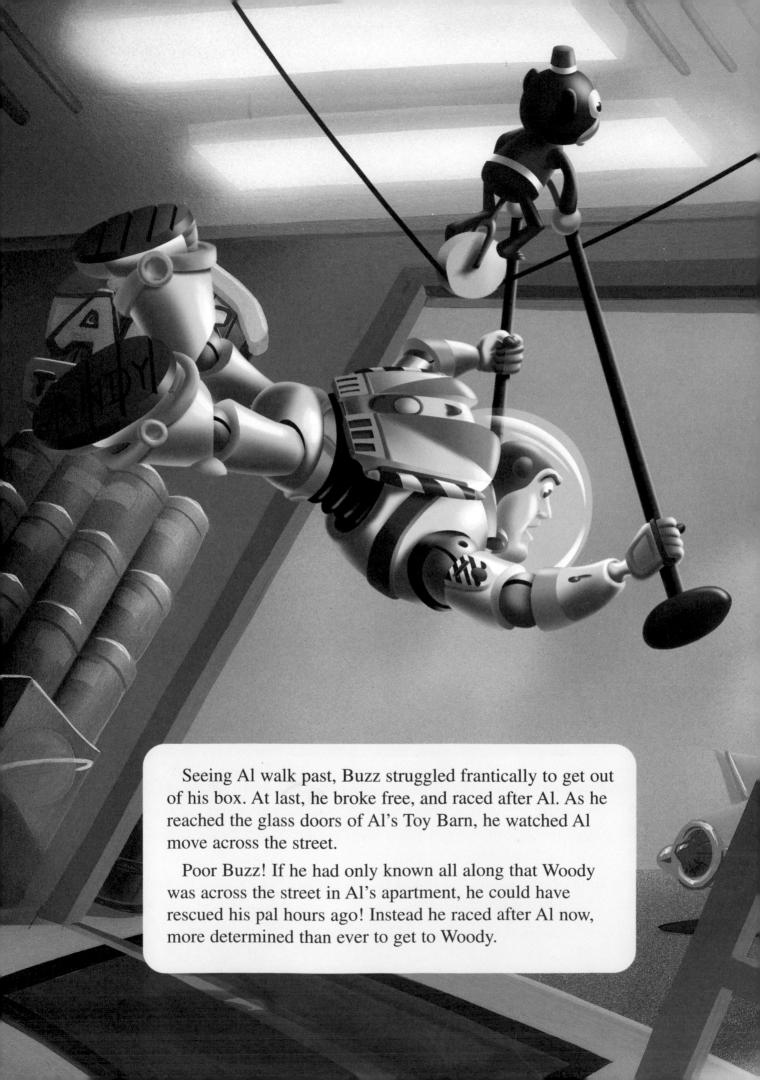

Seeing Al walk past, Buzz struggled frantically to get out of his box. At last, he broke free, and raced after Al. As he reached the glass doors of Al's Toy Barn, he watched Al move across the street.

Poor Buzz! If he had only known all along that Woody was across the street in Al's apartment, he could have rescued his pal hours ago! Instead he raced after Al now, more determined than ever to get to Woody.

As Buzz raced after Al's car, he never noticed that behind him, the evil Emperor Zurg, Buzz's arch enemy, stood in the doorway of Al's Toy Barn. The evil creature had broken free from his box and was now watching Buzz making his way to Al's apartment.

As soon as Al crossed the street, he parked his car in the driveway and then rode the elevator up to his apartment.

Much to their dismay, Andy's toys were left behind in the car. The toys quickly scrambled out of the car, but had no idea how to get up to Al's apartment.

Then New Buzz found a vent. 'Look!' he called. 'We can climb through here. It's like a tunnel going to the top.'

New Buzz clamped the magnets from the utility pack onto the vent's metal interior and dropped a line down for the other toys. Then they began climbing.

Luckily an elevator rose below them, catching them on its roof. As the toys rode it to the top of the building, they didn't realise that their true pal, Andy's Buzz, was clinging to the bottom.

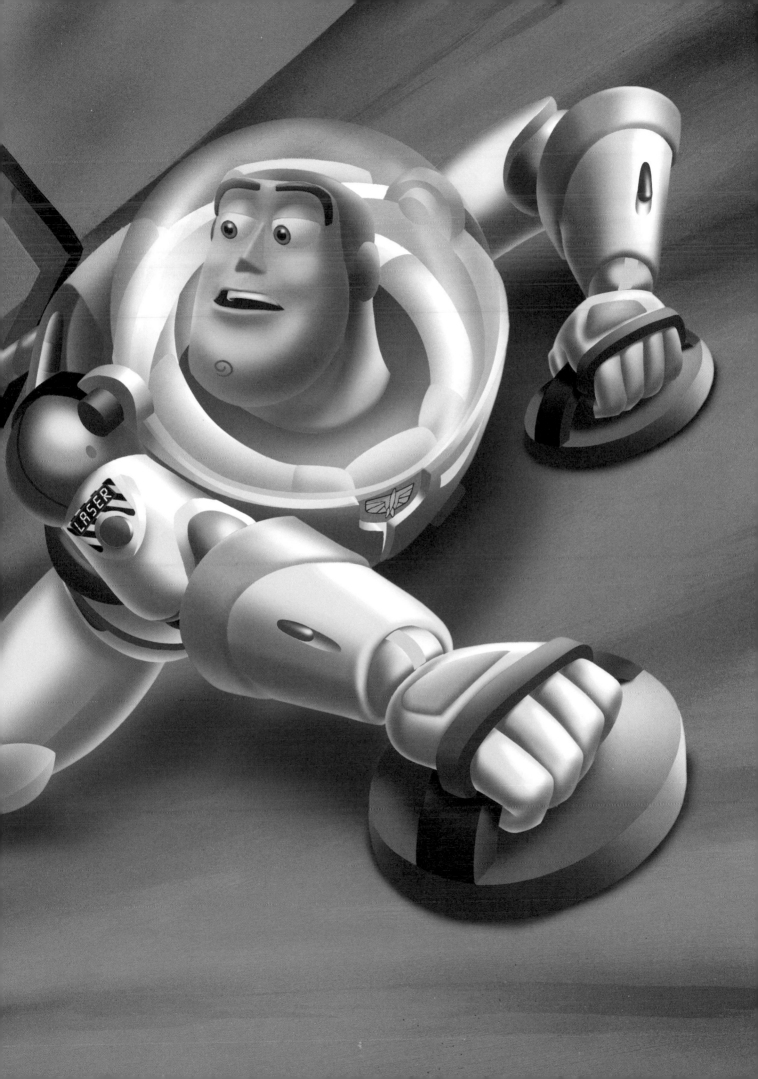

CRASH! Using Rex as a battering ram, the toys smashed through the vent into Al's apartment and confronted the Roundup toys.

Just then, Andy's Buzz burst into the room. Andy's toys gasped. There were two Buzzes! Which one was their friend?

As the others looked on in confusion, Buzz lifted his shoe, revealing Andy's name on the bottom. Andy's toys were shocked. They had been following the wrong Buzz!

Andy's Buzz ran up to Woody. 'Let's go!' he said.

'I can't, Buzz,' Woody said. 'I'm part of a rare collectible set. If I leave, these guys will spend the rest of their lives in storage. And, besides, one day Andy will just throw me away.'

'Woody, listen,' Buzz said. 'It's not about how long you last, but how much fun you give your kid. It's no good being a toy unless you're played with.'

But Woody wouldn't listen. At last, Buzz gave up and left.

Then Woody saw the TV Woody singing to a grinning little boy, and he realised how much he missed Andy. He knew he'd made a mistake. He decided to follow Buzz, and Jessie and Bullseye decided to go with him. 'Buzz! wait!' called Woody.

Just then, Al came in. He put the Roundup toys in his case and headed for the elevator.

Seeing this, Buzz ran through the vent, the other toys behind him, and jumped on top of the elevator roof. But Zurg was already there, waiting for them! With an evil laugh, he attacked the two Buzzes.

'I can't watch!' cried Rex, turning away. But as he did, his tail swung around and knocked Zurg off the roof!

Zurg was gone, but Woody still needed help. The toys peered through the roof into the elevator and saw Al standing beside the case containing Woody.

Quickly, the toys formed a long chain with Slinky at the end. Stretching his coils, Slinky managed to unlatch the case. But before he could grab his pal, the Prospector yanked Woody out of reach.

The elevator stopped, and Al stepped out. Slinky dangled forlornly in mid-air. Then he crashed to the floor, with his friends on top of him.

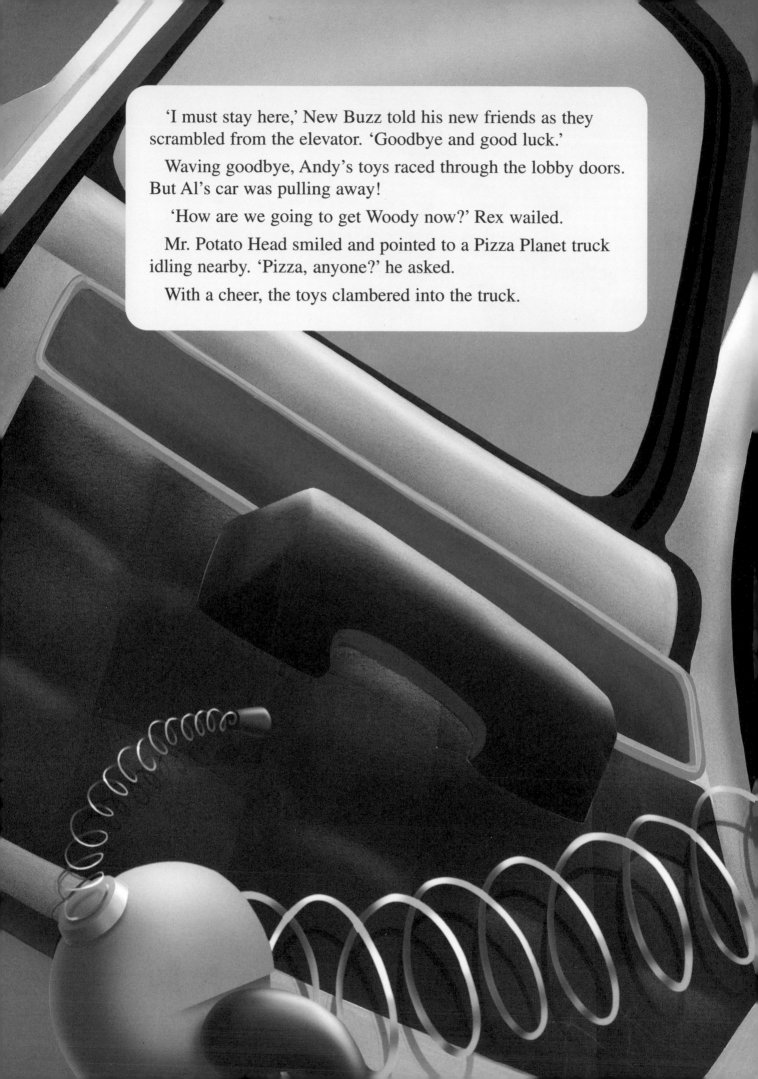

'I must stay here,' New Buzz told his new friends as they scrambled from the elevator. 'Goodbye and good luck.'

Waving goodbye, Andy's toys raced through the lobby doors. But Al's car was pulling away!

'How are we going to get Woody now?' Rex wailed.

Mr. Potato Head smiled and pointed to a Pizza Planet truck idling nearby. 'Pizza, anyone?' he asked.

With a cheer, the toys clambered into the truck.

Buzz climbed on top of a pile of pizza boxes to reach the steering wheel.

'Slink, take the pedals! Rex, you navigate. Hamm and Potato, operate the levers and knobs,' he commanded. The truck's lights flashed, the gas hatch flapped, the antenna zoomed, and the windshield wipers flipped. But the truck didn't move. Finally Buzz yanked the gear shift. With a grinding noise, the truck lurched and swerved into the street.

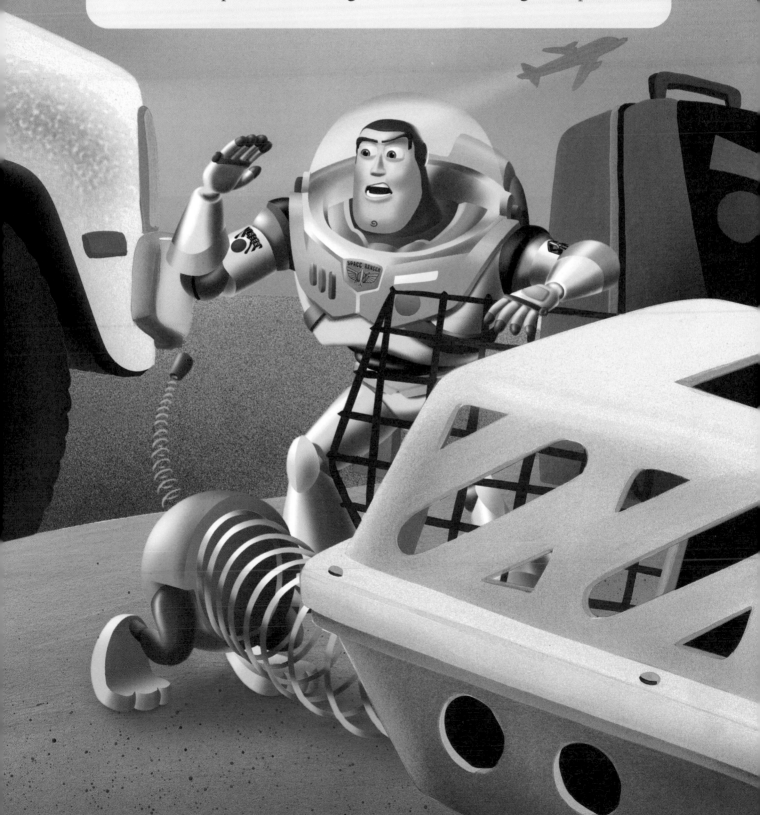

The Pizza Planet truck zigzagged through traffic, and at last, came to a shuddering halt beside the airport loading zone kerb. Al was already hurrying into the terminal with his cases.

Buzz glanced around the luggage loading zone and spotted a pet carrier near the terminal entrance.

'There's the perfect camouflage!' he shouted. 'Let's go, troops!'

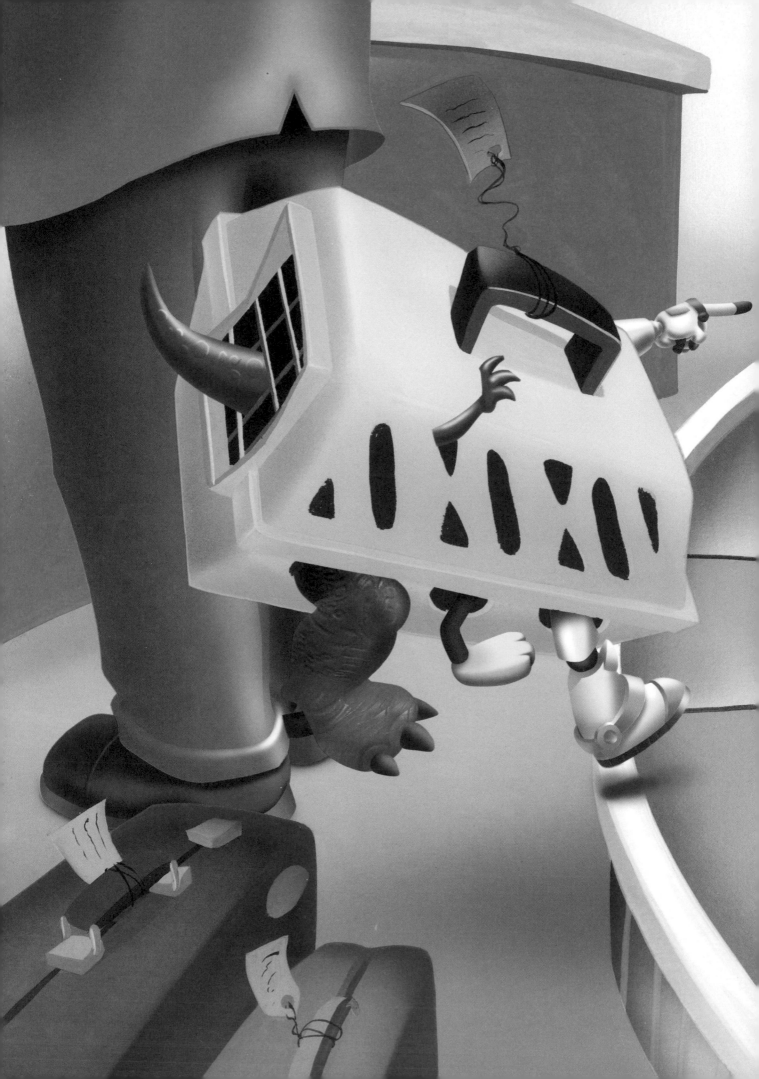

Moments later, the pet carrier scooted across the terminal, propelled by ten little toy legs.

The ticket agent yanked Al's case from his hand and thumped it onto the baggage conveyor belt.

Quickly, the toys in the pet carrier jumped onto the conveyor belt behind Al's case.

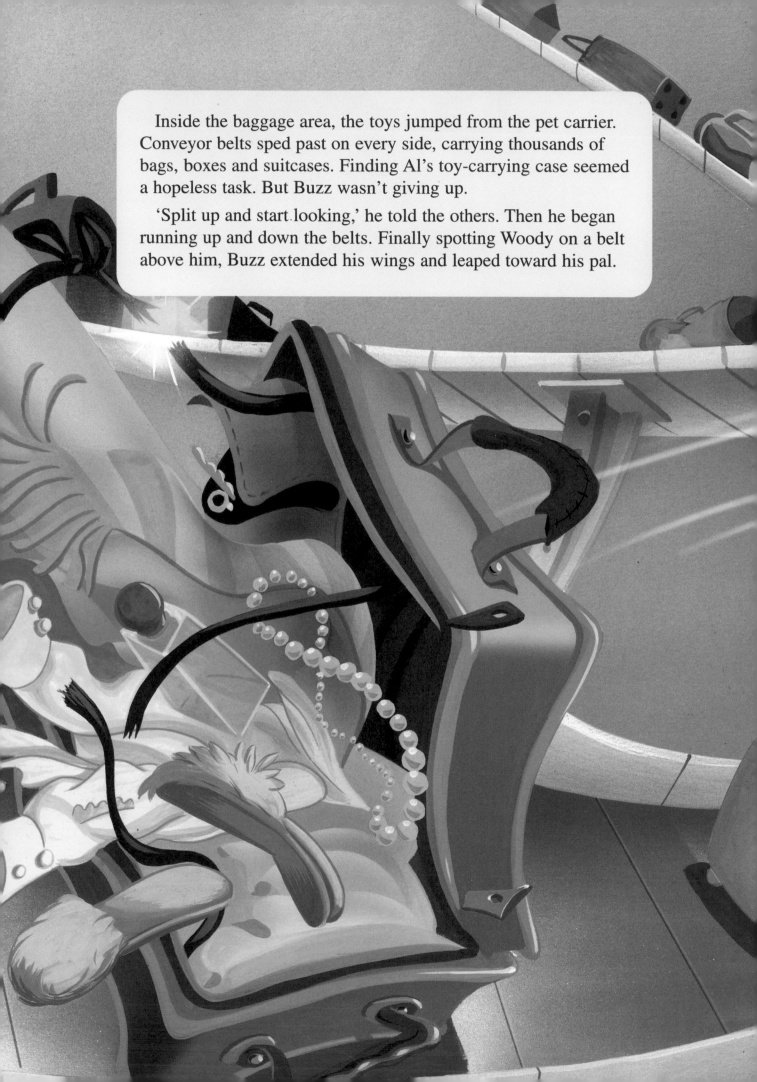

Inside the baggage area, the toys jumped from the pet carrier. Conveyor belts sped past on every side, carrying thousands of bags, boxes and suitcases. Finding Al's toy-carrying case seemed a hopeless task. But Buzz wasn't giving up.

'Split up and start looking,' he told the others. Then he began running up and down the belts. Finally spotting Woody on a belt above him, Buzz extended his wings and leaped toward his pal.

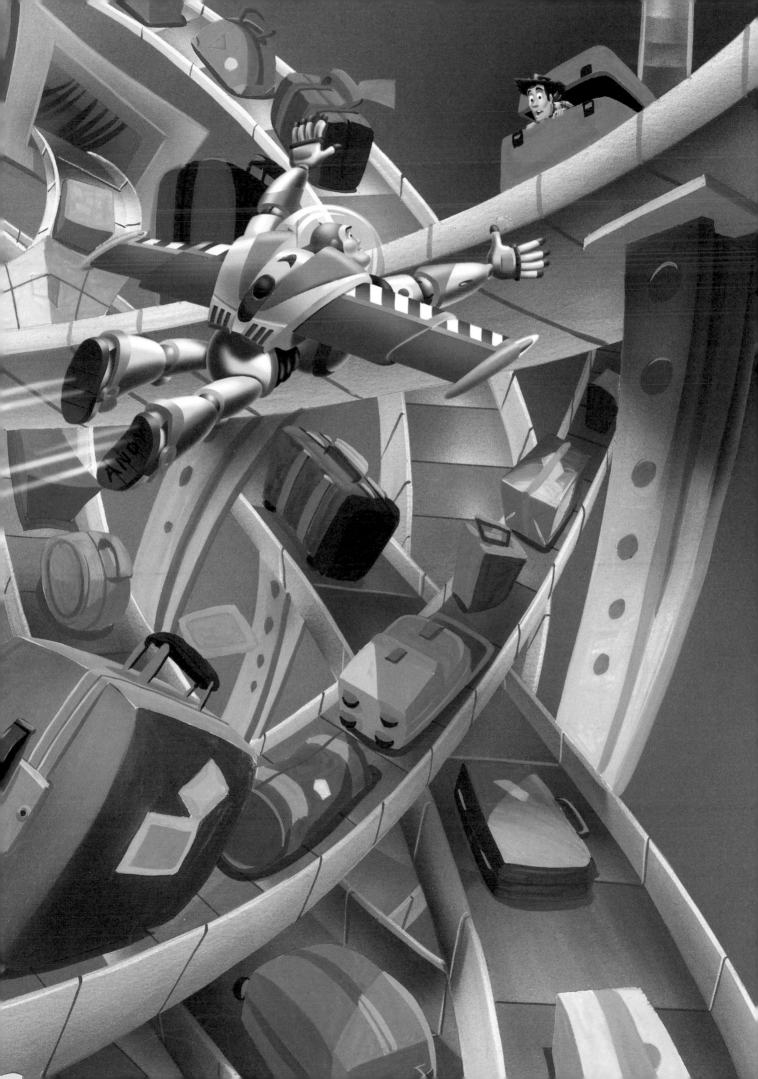

When Buzz reached Al's case and opened it, the Prospector leapt out and attacked him. He didn't want the Roundup toys to leave. He wanted them to stay as collectibles, not toys.

Woody climbed up the conveyor belts to where Buzz and the Prospector were fighting. Together, Woody and Buzz stuffed the struggling Prospector into a passing backpack.

Buzz and Woody grinned at each other. But there was no time to waste. Al's case was speeding down the belt toward the outdoor baggage carrier. In a few minutes it would be loaded onto the plane.

'We've got to get Bullseye and Jessie!' Woody exclaimed. As he and Buzz tore down the conveyor belt, they saw Bullseye struggle from the case. But Jessie was still inside!

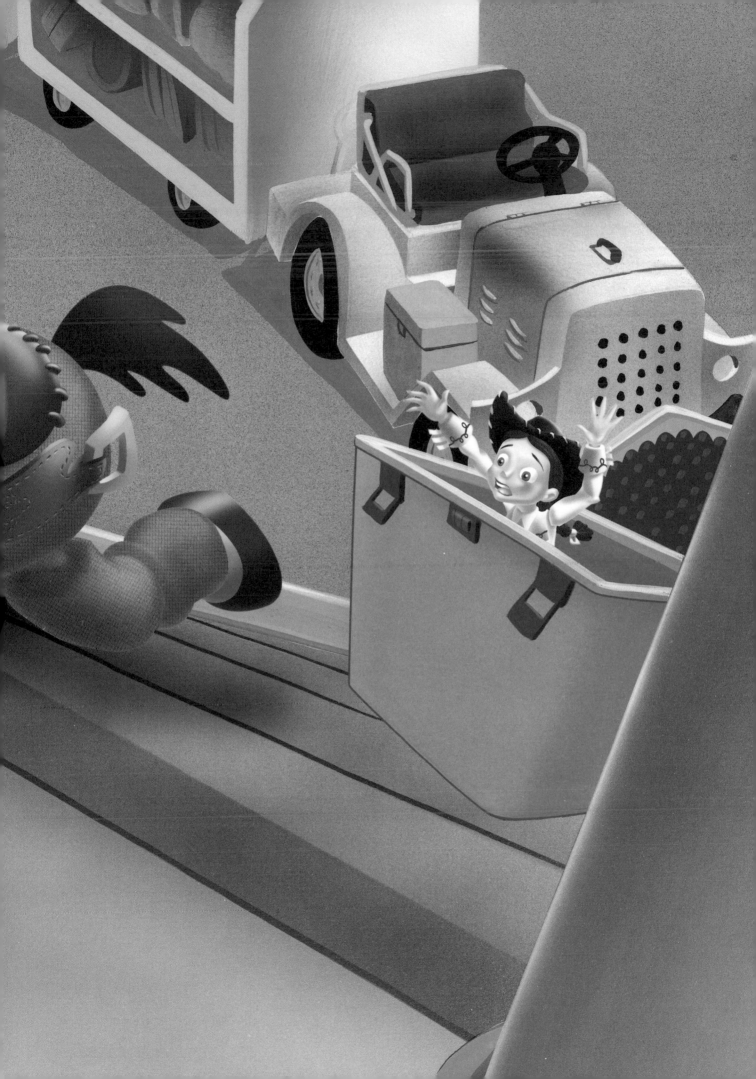

Woody flung himself onto Bullseye's back, pulled Buzz on behind him, and raced after the baggage train.

'Whoa!' Buzz yelled. 'I'm a space ranger, not a cowboy!'

'Watch this, Buzz!' Woody shouted as they galloped beside the train. 'I saw this on my television show!' He balanced on Bullseye's back, gave a loud YA-HOO, and leaped onto the speeding train.

Scrambling along the top of the bags, Woody searched for the case holding Jessie. Suddenly the baggage train pulled up beside the plane, and a baggage handler tossed Al's case into the cargo hold.

'I'm NOT letting Jessie down!' Woody thought. 'She deserves another chance to play with a kid who loves her.' He quickly jumped into a golf bag, just before it was loaded onto the plane.

'Oh, Woody, you're here!' Jessie exclaimed when Woody opened the case and helped her out. 'I'm so glad to see you!'

'Follow me!' Woody cried. 'We don't have much time left.' He led Jessie through the cargo hold to the escape hatch just over the plane's wheels.

But the plane was already beginning to move onto the runway.

As the two toys climbed down toward the wheel, Jessie slipped. Woody reached out to grab onto her when — RRRRIIPP! — his arm ripped. His grip grew weak, and Jessie slipped from the edge of the escape hatch. She dangled just inches above the churning wheels. Thinking quickly, Woody yanked his pullstring as far as it would go and lassoed Jessie with it.

At almost the same instant, Bullseye and Buzz galloped up to the wheels.

'Jump, Woody, jump!' Buzz shouted.

Holding Jessie tight with the last bit of strength in his arm, Woody jumped safely onto Bullseye's back. 'Yeeeeehaaaah!' he cried as his pullstring rewound.

A short time later, Andy and his mum arrived home.

'What is a baggage carrier doing parked on the street?' Andy's mum wondered as she pulled into the driveway. But Andy was too glad to be back to care.

Andy ran up the stairs, burst into his room, and grabbed Woody from the shelf. 'Howdy, pardner!' he exclaimed. 'Boy did I miss you!'

Then Andy spotted Bullseye and Jessie lying beside a plate of cookies. A sign on Etch-a-Sketch said 'Welcome Home, Andy!'

'New toys! Thanks, mum!' he shouted as he picked up Bullseye and Jessie. Then, to their delight, he began to play with them.

The next day, as soon as Andy left the room, the toys held their own special party. Jessie and Bullseye were happy as could be — not only were they together with Woody, but Andy loved playing with them. Even Wheezy was back, with his voice completely restored.

As for Woody and Buzz, they were just glad to be home in Andy's room where a toy was guaranteed to have fun...just playing.